What's Bugging You?

"You're Either On the Way, or In the Way"

What's Bugging You?

How to **Motivate Yourself** and Others Through Teamwork, Change, and Attitude!

Keith Harrell

An imprint of HPS Publishers

Designed by mudpie graphics, inc.
Dust jacket photo by Mark Squire Photography
Illustrations by Walt Floyd

Library of Congress Cataloging-in-Publication Data
has been applied for.

ISBN 978-0-9826101-0-7

Fourth Edition

To every championship team and to every winning athlete, thank you for inspiring me over the years. Thank you to all of my coaches, teammates, friends, and role models. I realize no one really wins . . . without teamwork.

To my motivational teacher, mentor and Christian Brother Zig Ziglar. Thanks a zillion, Zig, for your life-changing work. I first read your book See You At The Top *over twenty years ago and the truth from those pages has no doubt inspired me to be doing what I am today. You have blessed me more than you will ever know, and like thousands of others, I thank God for you.*

Also to my best buddy, Jeff Dowdle. Thanks for showing me how to live life with a million-dollar smile, a high level of enthusiasm, and a first-class attitude. We all miss you.

Contents

If you can't change your fate, change your attitude.

1
Opening

I wrote this book for your continuous improvement process to help you eliminate or better manage *What's Bugging You?* and to help you grow to an even higher level of both personal and professional success.

This simple (but powerful) parable is about a person whose life has been turned upside down. His wife is contemplating ending their twenty-one year marriage. The recent downturn in the economy has almost wiped out his 401k. His mortgage is in foreclosure, his health is being challenged by high blood pressure, high cholesterol, and a tremendous amount of stress. In addition, rumor has it that his company is on the verge of a major downsize.

So, *What's Bugging You?* Think about it, what are some of your challenges? This book was written to help you, or someone you know, overcome them by illustrating profound *truths* about attitude, change, and teamwork that encompass Guiding Principle Steps (GPS) and Be-Attitudes to enable individuals, teams, and organizations to navigate through and around everyday challenges. It also identifies the most common, ineffective (bad) attitudes that have been known to "bug" or challenge organizations, teams, and individuals all over the world.

For every individual who desires to achieve success, for every team and organization that strives to stay competitive and work as a team, it is essential to find the root cause of poor performance, discontent, and underachievement. And subsequently, to understand the action steps needed to embrace change, enhance morale, and improve performance.

Throughout this book you will be asked several questions to challenge your thinking and uplift your attitude. These questions, asked in slightly different ways than you're accustomed to, will hopefully lead you to new levels of insight. It's important to know that when you want better answers, you have to ask better questions.

Of all the books I've written, this one is very special to me. I've shared this story with countless people from all walks of life and professions, and it never fails to amaze me that each time they hear it, it is like a light has been turned on within. They begin to clearly see there is room for improvement in all of us.

Do you believe there is room for improvement in you?

How about room for improvement on your team? In your organization?

Where you are going is much more important
than where you have been.

2

Speech—Part 1
"The Journey"

The audience erupted in applause as Chris made his way to the front of the ballroom. His division's record-setting year had brought him here to accept the award on behalf of his team. Biting his lower lip and taking a deep breath to control the heartfelt emotion of the moment, Chris stood silently at the podium recalling everything that had led up to tonight's awards dinner. He scanned the crowd for a glimpse of the team members who had worked tirelessly with him to turn the company's weakest link into the strongest—those who had moved his department from "worst" to "first," nodding and giving the thumbs up to those he made eye contact with. There were a couple of scattered whistles and cheers before the noise finally died down.

As he took the microphone, Chris paused and

smiled. He couldn't help but think how different he was from the man he had been just a year ago. He was excited to share with his curious colleagues what everyone had been clamoring to find out ever since he had returned from his trip to Dallas—*the secret behind his personal transformation, and his team's tremendous success.* . . .

Are you playing to win . . .
or playing not to lose?

How different are you today
from the person you were
a year ago?

How could a personal
transformation improve
your success?

Change the way you talk about yourself
and begin to change your life.

3

Airport and the Scientist
(One Year Ago)

Chris scowled as he stood looking through the massive window at Gate A-27 in the Sea-Tac International Airport, where storm clouds were quickly rolling in. Being an experienced traveler, he knew the lightning would shut the flight down if they didn't get loaded and off the ground within a half hour. Not that he was in any hurry to get to Dallas, mind you. But he was already annoyed, and a delay was the last thing he needed this morning.

"Wow, it looks like we are going to get a lot of rain." An enthusiastic voice came from behind him.

Chris turned to see a grinning man with a newspaper tucked under his arm standing in front of him.

"Hello there . . . my name's Herman," he said.

Chris nodded in return.

"You know, the fire ants love to come out right after the rain. They're from Brazil, so I guess the rain forest is in their genes."

Chris turned back to stare out the wall of glass. Herman stepped up next to him. They both silently watched the airline workers scramble to get luggage on and off the planes before the storm drove them indoors.

"Do you live in Dallas, or are you going to visit?" Herman inquired, breaking Chris' concentration.

Chris saw he wasn't going to be able to get out of talking to Herman, so he turned to him. "Well, my company's headquarters is there and I have to meet with the human resources VP later this week. It's only the third time I've been there in 17 years."

Herman smiled. "Sounds exciting!"

Chris grimaced slightly and went on. "I could think of a lot of things I could call it. Exciting would not be one of them. I'm pretty sure I'm being called to the home office because they're planning to lay me off."

Herman responded softly, "Sorry to hear that, but how can you be so sure?"

"I'm the sales director for an IT company and business has been bad; my numbers have been on a steady decline for the past three years. Rumor has it, we may be downsizing. I've been with them for a lot of years, and I have to say, this really stinks," Chris said, a little surprised at how good it made him feel to vent about it.

"Un-huh, I see," nodded Herman.

"The way I've been treated the last few months is wrong. It's not my fault the numbers are down. I know there are a lot of people I can blame for this.

"My department has a high turnover rate and nobody stays around long enough to learn the product line in order to make their monthly quotas. We're losing our added value and our competitive advantage. We've always been able to differentiate ourselves by the quality of our people *and* by the quality of our products."

Herman's brows lowered as he listened intensely.

"Morale is terrible and nobody wants to work together and embrace the changes that are needed to help turn things around."

Herman was nodding his head sympathetically. "I understand teamwork and embracing change can be challenging at times," he said. "For people, anyway."

Chris looked puzzled. "What do you mean?"

"I mean there are many lessons we could learn from our friends the ants."

"They're a lot like people, but ants sure handle teamwork and change better than we do."

Chris frowned, wondering why he'd bothered to open up to this guy who obviously didn't understand the seriousness of his situation. *Ants? Is this guy serious?*

Unfazed, Herman continued, "Ants are so much like people—they live in colonies, we live in communities; there are all types of ants, and there are all types of people. Amazing creatures. They are resilient, self-sacrificing, and conscientious workers that accomplish feats that would be considered impossible if they were our size. For example, they're known to carry up to 50 times their weight!

"You know, it's not just what they do or how much

they can carry, it's their attitude while doing it.

"Do you remember the popular slogan that Nike came out with years ago?"

"Yeah, *Just Do It*," Chris responded.

"As human beings, we often have to be reminded to take action if we want to get things done," Herman continued.

"Ants never have to be told to *just do it* because they have a built-in attitude that enables them to *just be it!* They seem to have a *right-now attitude* to do whatever it takes to always get the job, assignment, or task done.

"Ego doesn't exist because they all share the same winning attitude, and that is, *if one wins, everybody wins.*"

"I've identified several, what I call *Be-Attitudes* that ants model throughout their lifetimes, which seem to be a framework that helps them to achieve their overall success."

"So you're trying to tell me ants actually think?"

"Most people underestimate their intelligence and their personal leadership skills. Regardless of their age, title, role, or status in life . . .

"they all accept their individual responsibility for leadership."

"They pride themselves on the fact that there's a leader that lives within all of them.

"The role of each ant changes throughout its lifetime. Watching and learning the jobs of older ants encourages them. If a colony gets into trouble, they'll all set aside their usual jobs and do whatever tasks are required to get through the crisis. Isn't that just brilliant?"

"I guess? But I don't have a *bug* problem, I have a *people* problem. And how do you know so much about ants, anyway?" he asked. Chris was somewhat irritated by Herman's enthusiasm. *How could anyone be so excited about pesky little ants?*

"I'm a myrmecologist," Herman replied. "You could call me an ant scientist. I've studied them for 30 years. I'm going to Dallas to be the keynote speaker at the Seventh Annual Global Warming Symposium. I will be talking about the long-term effects of climate change on ant behavior. It's important to realize that whatever is affecting them now will soon be affecting us . . . if it's not already.

"Like us, they're very sensitive, just much more adaptable. Ants are also creative thinkers and masters of innovation. They don't think outside the box—for them, *there is no box*. I'm so amazed by the human qualities they display that I never get bored talking about them."

"Obviously," Chris mouthed, to no one in particular.

Just then, the men were interrupted by a crackling announcement over the intercom informing them that Flight 1298 was ready to board.

Chris pulled out his ticket and grabbed his briefcase, relieved to be finished with the small talk and finally on his way.

The airline agent called each group by zone and urged everyone to get on board and quickly settled so they could depart before the storm moved in.

The boarding area came alive with people gathering coats, bags, and children as they streamed toward the gate.

Chris checked his watch, nodded to Herman, and made a quick dash to the restroom. Standing at the sink he looked into the mirror. *Boy, you look ten years older. Look at all of your wrinkles, and where did all of this gray hair come from? You feel like you look!* As he turned the corner to exit the men's room, a very tall, heavyset man ran right into him, knocking Chris off balance.

"I'm so sorry," the man quickly apologized. "I didn't see you."

"Watch where you're going," barked Chris.

"Hey, it was an accident," the man said defending himself. He then added sarcastically, *"What's Bugging You?"*

Chris thought, *"What's bugging me?"* And, for the next few minutes, the question played over and over in his head, until the answer became clear.

What was bugging Chris was more than just the fear of losing his job. The economy was bugging him. His marriage had hit a few more bumps than he cared to admit. Then there were the investments that had gone bad. And the health problems. No use in denying it any longer—he was in a tailspin.

When Chris finally got in line to board the plane, he was still thinking about the man's question, *"What's Bugging You?"*

What is your competitive advantage?

What is morale like on your team? What can you do to improve it?

So, *What's Bugging You?*

You can choose to change.

4
Takeoff

Boarding went quickly, with harried passengers stuffing briefcases and carry-on bags anywhere they would fit. Others squeezed by each other in the narrow aisle, hunting for the last pillows and blankets before buckling in for takeoff.

A very attractive woman toting a large green bag and a shrieking toddler was shaking her head apologetically as she slowly worked her way through the main cabin in front of Chris, who craned his neck to look past her and locate his seat.

Finally finding her seat, she struggled into her row, sat the child down, and began stuffing her belongings into the nearly filled overhead bin.

Chris checked his ticket again, and proceeded down the narrow aisle in search of his seat. When he looked up, there sat Herman, smiling from the window seat in his row.

He groaned inwardly over his awful luck.

"Well, can you believe this?" Herman beamed. "Looks like we'll have the whole three hours and fifty minutes to get to know one another!"

Chris gave a terse smile and tucked his laptop beneath the seat in front of him. "Great," was all he could muster as he settled in, fishing for his seat belt and shutting off his cell phone.

For the first time in all his years of flying, he clung to the hope that a middle-seat passenger would appear and fill the space between them—the bigger the person, the better—but the doors closed, leaving the men stranded together in row 17.

Chris sighed deeply, glancing at the surrounding rows for a vacant aisle seat as the flight attendant began her demonstration, but there weren't any.

Minutes later, the revved engines signaled takeoff, and quickly enough, Flight 1298 was airborne.

Chris reached for his paper and tried to appear preoccupied so Herman wouldn't attempt to engage him in further conversation, but it was a useless gesture. Herman continued where he'd left off, as if they had never been interrupted.

"You know, if you were an ant, life would be a lot

less difficult," Herman mused, in an apparent effort to cheer up his disinterested new friend.

"For ants, it's all about being *proactive*, *executing* and *getting results*. Simply put, if you were an ant, you would already know just what you're supposed to do, and everyone else would help you in whatever way you needed to get it done. Wouldn't that be great?"

Chris shrugged as the attendant's cart rolled by and little silver snack bags were dropped with napkins onto lowered tray tables.

He reflected a moment on Herman's last statement, before asking, "How smart can ants really be? Every time I see them, they're just running back and forth. Sometimes with food, and sometimes not. Sometimes in a line, and sometimes not. They seem pretty . . . *mindless*, if you ask me."

Herman leaned forward, as if on cue. "Ah, but what looks like random activity is actually highly sophisticated *synergy*. Everything they do has *purpose*. Individually, I think they're pretty remarkable—they never miss a beat as they carry out their daily tasks. It's when you step back and look at the big picture that you really appreciate the extraordinary world of ants.

"They have an innate ability to identify issues and

threats, and to resolve them before they escalate into a crisis.

"Their commitment is to the good of the team rather than putting their own needs first."

"Their investment is in each other.

"You probably wouldn't guess it, but their communication and organization skills—why, they're *legendary*! Their 'group intelligence' is so ingenious that business models have been built using ants' self-organizing ways. This particular behavior—called Swarm Intelligence—has been used in software applications to optimize business algorithms and solve computing problems. Everyone from moviemakers in Hollywood and financial firms to NASA and the military use this ant 'wisdom' in their applications.

"It's all pretty exciting, isn't it?" chuckled Herman, amused by the cleverness of his research subjects.

Chris managed a nod.

"And that simple sophistication is only part of why their system works so well. The intelligence is both inside and outside the group. That is, the ants each make decisions from a basic *diversity of thought*, yet their individual problem-solving creates a collective 'combined intelligence' to reach optimal results. That way, the best and the brightest solutions emerge naturally."

Herman paused to wash down a handful of peanuts with a gulp of apple juice and continued on, not noticing Chris' yawns.

"They seem to have tapped into a powerful, yet mysterious, ability to always embrace change with a *no-fear attitude*. They move and work together so seamlessly you'd think they were all getting instructions from the same brain. Now, maybe you don't think that's such a big deal, but then you don't know how big these super ant colonies can get.

"Want to take a guess? Think you'll even come close?" Herman asked, not expecting a response from his neighbor, who'd reclined his seat back and was resting his eyelids.

"Why, the largest colony in the world runs 3,600 miles from Northern Spain to the Italian Riviera! It has millions of colonies with several billion ants, and it's the single largest example of cooperation at work that you can find anywhere on the earth today."

Herman sighed, self-satisfied. "So, how do they do it, Chris? How do the ants manage to run these vast organizations so flawlessly when in your typical organization many people find it difficult to cooperate with someone in the same *department*? . . . Chris . . . you've been awfully quiet. Am I boring you with too many details?"

Chris responded with a grunt and a whistling snore.

Herman looked over and saw that Chris had fallen fast asleep. He stared for a moment, and smiled. Scratching his head, he settled back into his seat and finished off his bag of peanuts before opening up the sports section of his paper.

Chris shifted into a more comfortable position, and sank deeper into a sound sleep.

Are you coachable?

Is your commitment
to the good of your team?
To your organization?

Who are you mentoring
and coaching?

Dream to be more than you are.

5
Dream

Chris heard the screechy sounds coming from the other side of an office door across the room. His heart pounded as he sat up and blinked his eyes. *Where am I?* he wondered. *Whose voices are those?*

He didn't have to wait long to find out. A quick knock, and the door burst open. What Chris saw next almost gave him a heart attack.

A huge, life-size female ant came bursting in the door with a couple of phone messages and an official-looking memo. Her black compound eyes scanned him briefly as she nodded and placed the papers on his desk.

Chris hesitantly leaned forward to get a better view of the document the lady ant had placed before him. The memo was brief: The senior management team had scheduled a meeting for the following morning, and Chris was required to attend.

She stepped back and started for the door, then stopped and turned toward him again. "Oh, and Connie the Consult-ant called again about this year's survey results. She's been trying all week to reach you.

"The senior management team has been meeting every day since the reports came in. There are some highly unusual variances in the workers' feedback. Seems some disturbing patterns have emerged. Connie said to make sure you talk to her before you leave today."

Still stunned, Chris stared in disbelief at the life-sized ant, then looked down as he nervously smoothed his tie. A second wave of shock hit him as he caught sight of his own arm, because it was now actually a *leg*. Instead of a human arm reaching out from under his favorite Armani suit, Chris was looking at a hairy, brown, stick-like appendage in its place.

He fought to keep his composure. I am an ant, too?

What in the blazes is going on here?

Chris gripped his pen tighter. *Don't panic! Don't panic!* He gulped slowly and looked back up at the bizarre creature waiting for a response. She adjusted her dark blue skirt and coughed. "Is there something wrong, sir?"

He caught sight of his business card holder, and suddenly, it all made sense.

Chris knew why he was there, and he even knew who she was. He couldn't really say how or why he knew, but he somehow knew everything as he sat there at his desk.

He was the head of the Human Resources Department, and the ant colony he worked for had just completed its annual Employee Opinion and Satisfaction Survey. Although he had hired a consultant to work on this year's questionnaire, he had gotten so busy with a recent colony crisis that he had put off getting back to her for over a week.

Since the employee responses were predictable from year to year, he personally felt there was no real reason to think there would be any surprises this time around. Yes, a few issues had cropped up here or there, but certainly nothing could be as important as the engineering crisis, so he had let her messages wait.

"No—no, of course not, Barbara," he muttered. "Thanks. Could you get Connie on the phone?"

Barbara nodded crisply. "She's on hold. I'll put her through," she said, and scurried out.

Chris sat back in his swivel chair and thought about the implications of the memo. A deep sigh crept out as he recalled his last few conversations with the consult-ant.

Connie had been working with each of the department managers for weeks to complete her report before submitting the employee data to the senior management team. She had called again yesterday to discuss some of the latest news with him, but he had been too busy to get back to her.

Barbara buzzed to let him know Connie was on line one.

He picked up the phone and spun around in his chair taking in his new surroundings.

"Connie! Good to finally connect with you. So what is the general opinion of the organization these days? Will we make it another year?" he joked.

There was an awkward silence on the other end for a moment, and then Connie spoke. "Actually, Chris, that's the problem—if the Opinion Survey is any indication, we are headed in the wrong direction—and fast. Global warming, food shortages … Did you know that Food Share is down 20 percent and that there is increased competition coming from everywhere? And that's just what we're dealing with from the outside. Inside the colony, in addition to the engineering crisis, we've got some problems. We have begun an unprecedented tailspin and many in the colony may *not* make it another year."

"It looks like fear could be spreading throughout the organization."

Chris responded more soberly. "What? I knew we had some problems in the colony, but come on, is it really *that* bad?"

He squinted at the framed photograph on his desk, carefully studying each ant's face, trying to figure out which of the couples in the group beach shot could possibly be him and his wife.

Connie continued. "The issues that came up might not have been considered so grave had they surfaced at any other time, but you know that the colony is going into the most critical season of the year."

Her words and serious tone jolted Chris, who had heard there were complaints and rumors about downsizing, but felt everyone was overreacting. Although he knew that the negative feedback was unusual, he hadn't really given the bigger picture much thought. But now he realized the implications of what Connie was saying. "So what exactly is going on? What are the details?"

"There's a meeting first thing tomorrow morning. Did you get the memo?"

"Yes, I did." He glanced at the clock on the wall. "Hmmm, I didn't realize it was so late. I have a couple of errands to run, so I guess I can wait until then to get the full story."

"Okay, I think it'll be a long day, so we'd both better get some rest. I'll see you in the morning."

Chris hung up and sat at his desk for a moment. He popped a couple of antacids, then grabbed his coat and briefcase and headed out the door not exactly sure of his destination, but instinctively knowing he'd get there.

In your general opinion,
how are things going on your
team? In your organization?

Could fear be spreading
throughout the team?
Has fear infected you?

You have to be willing to pay the price.

6
Assignment

Chris looked around the table at the senior management team responsible for keeping everything running smoothly in the colony. He braced himself as the normally unruffled leader of the colony, known as "The Chairman," waved a thick stack of papers and leaned toward him, antennae waving wildly.

"Not good. Not good at all, Chris. Do you realize how bad it is right now? Food shortages, increased competition. It's a tough environment. There appears to be a small group, who are becoming like a cancer to our colony," The Chairman huffed.

Connie, the consult-ant, spoke up. "As you know, my team spent all last week going through the annual Employee Opinion and Satisfaction Surveys. Well, some very troubling information showed up. Most of the colony is concerned—over half of the employees gave the job opportunities, work climate, and future outlook a 63 percent satisfaction rating. That's down almost 20 percent from last year.

Leaning forward, The Chairman sighed. "And now this recent engineering disaster . . . The news had come as a shock to us. That is, until we received the summaries of the annual surveys. Last week's tunneling overshot—the first in our history—made more sense when the surveys confirmed some serious breakdowns going on in the organization. We aren't sure yet *how*, *why*, or *where* it all started."

Chris and Connie fidgeted in their seats.

"It seems that a surge in the ranks of unhappy ants has occurred this year and our quality assurance standards have bottomed out. But most disturbing is the fact that this growing wave of discontentment is not random. The trouble has been tracked back to a small group of ants," The Chairman stated.

Connie, interrupted him.

"They're not ants . . . why, they're aints!

Ain't responsible for any trouble as far as they're concerned."

"Yet, over and over again, their names came up in the comments section of the Employee Opinion and Satisfaction Surveys, as managers and co-workers repeatedly identified them as one of the main reasons that operations have fallen apart this year."

The Chairman cleared his throat. "In reading the surveys, you can clearly see that there are a handful of them who have been turning the colony upside down with their negative attitudes and disruptive activities. The problem is, their attitudes aren't just hindering their own personal progress. They are affecting many others who have been happy, productive workers in the past. Right now morale is at an all-time low, deadlines are being missed, and projects left unfinished in several strategic departments. We can't continue like this. The survival of the colony itself is at stake. We must do something about it at once because it's all about *selfishness* and *bad attitudes*, and the aints themselves are the source.

Both Chris and Connie nodded.

"Poisoned attitudes are contagious."

"They spread like a virus through the organization. All it takes is one ant to shut down communication or to decide his or her own agenda is more important than everyone else's. If we lose *faith* in our guiding principles, our mental toughness deteriorates, and our team dynamics drastically shift. If this worst case scenario was to happen, we'd then lose the master keys to success and our survival would be in jeopardy. Chris, you've got to get a handle on this before everything else unravels."

The Chairman paused long enough for Chris and Connie to absorb the seriousness of the situation.

"After thoroughly reviewing the survey data and the key issues regarding these—these *aints*—the senior management team has determined that each one of them has repeatedly violated the Guiding Principle

Steps and Be-Attitudes of the colony. All of the aints were given a plan and a goal. They still failed—even after a lengthy process of feedback and solutions, and prioritizing problematic areas, and agreeing on appropriate action plans to help re-engage them to the colony's Guiding Principle Steps and Be-Attitudes. Therefore, their managers were alerted to this earlier in the week, and they sat down with each of the aints to try to work through the complaints against them and find out what their responses might be.

"Some of them had been on probation at one point in the past year and were offered extra training and coaching, in hopes that one of these options might help get them off the destructive path they were on. Only one of the aints was slightly interested, but none of them took advantage of any of the options.

"One aint, however, did complain that his manager was handling things poorly. He has appealed to higher management and will be interviewed further. So, other than the one aint who has appealed, they have left us no choice but to release them immediately. Our priority now is to *restore confidence*, and bring optimum productivity back to the colony. Am I making myself clear?"

Chris and Connie nodded.

"Chris, I want you to meet with each of the aints immediately, along with their managers, to finalize the terminations and then to prepare a full report for the Board on how this happened in the first place. And, be sure to spell out for me the difference between an *ant* and an *aint*. We have no time to lose, so I expect you to have everything completed by the end of the workday."

Chris was stunned by the thought of having to do everything within the span of a day. He opened his mouth to respond, "But—"

The Chairman stood up signifying that the meeting was over, and Chris' objection got drowned out by the noise as the rest of the team got up, gathered their belongings, and followed their leader—all the while giving Chris sympathetic, but somber looks, as they filed out the door.

Chris rose to his feet and picked up the folder containing the survey results. His head was spinning with all the information they had gone over, and now he was expected to meet with the aints before the day's end, which didn't leave much time to prepare.

As he walked back to his office, he read one of the many colorful GPS (Guiding Principle Steps) and Be-Attitudes posted throughout the plant:

Teamwork—Live the Vision. Be Supportive.

Some of the other GPS and Be-Attitudes were:

Accountability— Say No to the Blame Game	Be Accountable
Ethical Execution— Do What's Right Because it's Right	Be Performance- and Integrity-Driven
Embrace Change— Convert Turning Points to Learning Points	Be a Change Embracer
Commit to Win— Do More Than is Expected	Be Coachable
Awareness — Notice What's Needed and Do What's Necessary	Be Responsible
Attitude is Everything— If Something is Wrong, Make it Right	Be the Difference

The signs were everywhere, and more than once he had heard employees repeating the words of wisdom in both department meetings and private discussions. For them, these weren't slick slogans. They were more than a flavor of the month, they were the culture and the fabric of the colony.

Just then, two young worker ants passed by laughing and joking with one another. Chris caught himself smiling as he watched them walk all the way to the end of the hallway and turn the corner. For a fleeting moment, he reflected on how interesting it was that attitudes—whether good *or* bad—were equally contagious.

As his office came into view, Chris sighed as an unexplainable heaviness settled on him. To have ants in the colony who *didn't* want to grow, to learn, to support one another? Ants who didn't want to *cooperate* with each other? Chris struggled with the concept. He had built his own reputation on helping others find their paths to success. He didn't—no, *couldn't*—understand why these unhappy workers rejected the satisfaction enjoyed by their co-workers in accomplishing great things beyond themselves. *Teamwork* had made the colony they worked for truly great, and it had become the envy of the entire region. It had been built on years of open communication, respect between workers and management, the latest in technology, and generous employee benefits. Other ants were constantly trying to transfer in from near and far.

He wondered how the recent events had gotten to such drastic levels. He also wondered whether other colonies were experiencing the same problems. But most of all, Chris wondered what it was that had made good ants go bad.

Attitudes are contagious.
Is yours worth catching?

You can be in the problem,
but the problem doesn't have to be in you.

7
Aints

Chris walked into his office and closed the door. He sat down and opened the folder, instantly overwhelmed by the amount of data he needed to go over before meeting with each of the aints and their managers.

He started with the high points of the annual Opinion Surveys, encouraged by the results from some of the most devoted ants in the colony. They gave high marks to everything from the availability of solid job opportunities, to the simplest things, like the quality of nectar dispensed by the new honeypot vending machines.

They were challenged by their job descriptions, but not overwhelmed.

They were identified as great mentors by the younger ants.

And they were creative in their solutions to obstacles that came up in daily operations.

Chris smiled as he read workers' remarks in the comments sections of several of the surveys. Many expressed excitement about their department successes and listed examples of combining resources to come up with better procedures and methods for defense and food gathering.

He was glad that he started with the year's victories and advances, because right now, he needed to be reminded that there were many superior aspects to his colony and reasons to be proud of the ants that made it so. In general, he was encouraged by the majority of the comments in front of him.

He continued working down through the stack as the scores descended, and saw, to his disappointment, that there were far more negative surveys than he had ever seen in past years. He flipped through several of them and found the tone became increasingly harsher with each one he read. A few were almost painful to read; they were so filled with anger toward supervisors and co-workers or mockery of management decisions. Each time he saw a survey that identified ants by name as department or colony problems, he pulled it and placed it in a separate pile.

He finished the first round of survey results, took a break and got a cup of Starbucks before going back and diving into the source of the colony's growing problems. (Ants like Starbucks, too? Who knew?)

He read each of the surveys, shaking his head as he went over the countless comments by disgruntled workers whose unhappiness was spreading like a contagion throughout the organization. He began to see a pattern emerging.

Every incident, complaint or problem seemed to point to the same three employees.

No wonder the senior management team had no problem tracing the colony's recent operation break-downs to the attitudes of these aints. It was all documented in black and white.

He placed Connie's report on the desk in front of him, noting the code names she had inked in next to each of the primary pessimists names:

Free Agent—*Aint on the Team*

Faultfinder—*Aint to Blame*

Change Resister—*Aint Changing*

They were from various levels, but he was familiar with each one of them, including their followers—some were basic worker ants, others were supervisors or managers. A small group of aints, they were affecting operations on a wide scale. He finished reading the survey information, jotting down questions and last-minute notes as he prepared to meet individually with each worker and their manager.

Finally, he was ready.

He gave Barbara his schedule and asked her to call ahead to the various departments as he started the walk toward his first meeting with Free Agent and his manager, Ant-alytical Ed, down in Engineering.

What makes you proud
to be part of your team?
Your organization?

What victories have you
experienced this year?

Are you unhappy or
disgruntled?

8

Code Name: Free Agent
Aint on the Team

"I'm telling you, it's never happened before. The point of intersection was missed by ten feet! *Ten feet!*" The Engineering Department manager's eyes were bulging and his face looked like it was going to explode.

"This is unbelievable! The other team followed specifications perfectly—they were right on target, and exactly on schedule. But Free Agent was handling the blueprints for his team and somehow got hold of a different set of prints. Without getting approval, he decided to take a shortcut and make some unauthorized changes. So now, we have two perfectly drilled segments of a 'tunnel to nowhere.' The entire tunneling operation has been set back by weeks. And this isn't the first time we've had problems with him. I've warned

Free Agent over and over again about his attitude. He thinks that because he's won a couple of engineering awards that he knows everyone else's job better than they do, that he doesn't have to play by the same rules as everyone else, or even work with the team at all. He's thrown co-workers under the bus more than once when projects derailed or fell behind schedule.

"Well, I've let him get away with his 'star status attitude' for too long—this time, it's really going to cost us. Everything is on hold until we fix this—we won't be ready to receive food until the two tunnel sections have been remapped and connected. I've sent five new teams in, but the ground is already firming up, so it's going slower. And there's the danger of increased predatory activity out there. I have no clue if we're going to be able to pull this off in time."

Chris tried to calm the manager down. "I understand your frustration, Ed. And unfortunately, he's not the only threat to our winter operations. Free Agent was just one on a short list of employees whose destructive attitudes and behaviors came up repeatedly in the latest Employee Opinion and Satisfaction Survey.

"For the first time, we're seeing exactly how quickly poor attitudes can translate into poor performance."

"And believe me, the situation is far worse than any of us realized. Seems they have degraded every operation they have a connection with. It also appears they are determined to bring others down with them. The Board has charged me with getting to the bottom of things and turning the situation around immediately, so I have a lot to do today. I'll need to meet with you and Free Agent as soon as possible, so if he's around now—"

"No," Ed replied. "He's ten minutes over on his break, again. If you wouldn't mind going to get him while I make a quick call, that would really help me out."

"No problem." Chris started walking toward the break room, stopping briefly as he always did to admire the Leaf Processing Department, where the Leafcutter ants brought the massive green sheets to be broken down and prepared for the gardens where food would be grown for the colony. He liked to stop by when he could, just so he could watch them at work, busily cleaning the leaves and cutting them into small pieces. He was always awed by the precision and speed of the workers as they handled the raw materials that kept the colony supplied with food.

But today, something was wrong. The ants were all there, but not one of them was working. Everything was at a standstill, with some ants pacing back and forth while others just sat around looking anxious. Chris was confused for a moment, and then suddenly realized why they were idle. Their department was waiting on the leaves from the foraging teams, who were behind on their quotas due to the engineering miscalculation. Even the scouts were wandering aimlessly, since it didn't make any sense to locate more food when the teams couldn't transport what was already found. The effects were rippling through the *entire* organization. Chris felt an uneasiness come over him as he was reminded of the urgency of his mission. He walked on, making a mental note to stop at the Architectural Department after he spoke with Free Agent to check on a hunch he had regarding some of the details.

His pace slowed as he approached the break room. He heard a lot of noise, including several loud voices and a burst of screechy laughter as he opened the door. On the far wall was evidence of a recent food fight, as some noodles were still making a slow slide down to the floor. Everything got quiet as multiple sets of large black eyes all stared at him.

Chris asked if anyone had seen Free Agent.

"Who wants to know?" came the belligerent reply from someone in the crowd.

Chris identified himself, and Free Agent poked his head around one of the other ants. "Here I am," he said with a sneer. "What can I do for you, Mr. HR?"

"I believe your break is over by more than a few minutes, and I'd like to sit down with you and your manager. Would you mind heading back with me to your department?"

Chris ushered him out as the room resumed its activity in noisy speculation of what the interruption might be about. They walked back toward the Engineering Department and passed a large window overlooking the beautiful sand sculptures outside.

Once they returned and everyone got seated back in Ed's office, Chris explained his mission and didn't waste any time getting to the point.

"Free Agent, I'm not sure you realize the number of times your manager has covered for you when you went against instructions because you thought your ideas were better than what had been decided by the organization.

"And I'm not sure if you know how many other employees have complained about you leaving them stuck in the middle of critical situations or not caring about the welfare of your team when things get tough and you're up against hard circumstances. Your *inability to be a team player* has affected everyone's performance including your own, and that's why you don't have a lot of fans around here."

Free Agent snickered. "Yeah, well, they say it's lonely at the top."

Ant-alytical Ed, shook his head. "This isn't a joke, Free Agent. You know we've talked about this too many times. Maybe if just once, you had thought about the team first and realized how much we depend on you—depend on each other—we wouldn't be in this situation right now.

"Everyone on this team knows their role, and how their role helps the team reach its goal. Our department has always based its success on strong teamwork, with everyone respecting each other, sharing their gifts and talents, and working as a team. The foundation of our teamwork has always been built on *truth*, *trust*, and *good communication*. Your biggest problem is you don't communicate; your teammates don't trust you, and you seldom tell the truth!"

Chris agreed. "You may be lonely, but it's not because you're at the top. It's because you refuse to be a team player."

Free Agent shot Chris an angry look. "I'm so sick of everyone saying that! What team? While working at my last colony I was burned a couple of times by so called, 'teammates.' I've learned that if you want something done right, you do it yourself. This whole teamwork culture in my opinion is overrated. It's just a job, and I'm one of the most skilled workers in this department."

Ed stood up and pointed his two top legs at Free Agent, "You are not the only ant who has been disappointed, or 'burned' as you call it. What happened to you is simply called 'life.'

"When life knocks you down, it doesn't have to knock you out. You can be the victim or the victor!"

"As ants, it's in our DNA to never cave in, give up, or quit. We never stop supporting the team, and we never stop being a team player, no matter what!"

Chris jumped in. "Free Agent, nobody's questioning your talent. It's your *selfish ambition* that is hurting all of us. Your personal agenda has put the entire colony in peril. There is no *'I'* in team.

"Your latest demonstration has resulted in an unprecedented fiasco—the worst tunneling error in our history—which has disrupted colony operations across the board. Thousands of ants had to be pulled off their usual assignments and are now working day and night trying to fix your mistake. And your timing couldn't have been worse. Coming right before the winter it will likely impact the lives of over a third of our population, since the food needed for the hatching eggs won't be there, and the less hardy ants won't survive without a steady food supply. How could you have done such a thing to your team—to the future of our colony?"

Free Agent hunkered down and crossed his two top legs. "Hey, don't be laying a guilt trip on me. I thought I had found a great shortcut to save some time and finish the tunnel ahead of schedule, that's all. I thought using a better set of plans would let me meet up with the other team sooner. If it had worked, everyone would be calling me a hero instead of blaming me. I was only trying to expedite the process, and it turns out the plans I used were wrong. Okay, so I made a bad call. Are you saying an ant can't make a mistake around here?"

"It's good you took a risk, but you took it with the wrong motive. And in the aftermath, you've taken *no accountability*. This isn't just about making mistakes." Chris wanted to make sure Free Agent realized the consequences his rebel decision had on all of them. "It's much more important than that; it's about a *mindset*. It's about an attitude and a choice to see yourself and your agenda as more important than anything else, including the safety and good of the team. This time, they'll have to pay an especially high price for your personal ego trip."

Free Agent fidgeted under the glare of the light that was being placed on his recent actions, as Chris wondered if any of what they were saying might be getting through.

He paused to wait for Free Agent's response.

"Well, I don't see it the same way. Nobody's looking out for me, so I have to do that for myself. I think you have to make your own way in this world, and hope for the best regardless of who gets hurt."

Chris looked at the aint with disappointment. He knew change had to start internally, and that Free Agent could not be expected to change if he saw nothing wrong with what he had done.

"Free Agent, explain to me how you reconcile your actions while ignoring GPS 1 and the corresponding Be-Attitude."

The blank look made Chris realize that Free Agent didn't even know which GPS and Be-Attitude he was referencing, even though all ants were required to memorize the principles early in their training. GPS 1: *Teamwork—Live the Vision. Be supportive!* "Free Agent, do you even have a clue? Living the vision is what fuels our success, it's what keeps us ants from burning out. First things first—Number 1: You must know the vision. Number 2: You must live it. And, that's done by doing Number 3: Connecting your personal vision to the colony's vision.

"Do you remember your personal vision? A personal vision always starts with . . . What do you want to do, for whom, and for what purpose?

"Free Agent, look at me. . . . When you fail to connect your personal vision to the colony's vision, that's when we all lose.

"By the way, do you understand what the Be-Attitude to *be supportive* means? Who have you supported lately? Free Agent, have you ever supported anyone?"

Free Agent wouldn't look Chris in the eye.

Chris knew he wasn't getting anywhere. *Connie was right*, he thought. *This guy just "aint on the team."*

"Free Agent, you know what it means to violate the GPS of the colony. Your manager has tried to give you the benefit of the doubt and overlook your failure to meet colony rules time and time again, and you were given many opportunities to change. Over the last year you have been on and off probation several times. Even after a lengthy process of feedback and suggested solutions, prioritizing problematic areas, and agreeing on appropriate action plans to try to help re-align your thinking with our GPS and Be-Attitudes . . . you still failed!

"We've run out of excuses for your continual disregard for your teammates and the colony vision. There's just no room for an ant who doesn't want to live the vision and refuses to connect his personal vision with the organization's. You've continually refused to be part of the team we are trying to build here. Time's up. It's gotten too dangerous to allow your attitude and behavior to remain in our operation."

There was an awkward silence. Several minutes passed before Chris shook his head and stood up. Obviously, the meeting was over.

He thanked them both, picked up his folder and handed Ed a thin stack of paperwork to go over with Free Agent, and left the room.

Teamwork is built on truth, trust, and good communication.

Are you a genuine team player?

Bitter or better? Victim or victor? How do YOU handle disappointment?

9

Code Name: Faultfinder
Aint to Blame

Chris heard them before he saw them. As he rounded the corner, they were already in a heated exchange that was escalating quickly. As far as he could tell, their argument revolved around the department's latest expedition, where one of the younger scouts apparently left a scent trail that had led several foraging groups right into a pesticide trap.

Chris approached them but they were too engaged to notice him as he walked up.

"I *know* I was leading the group, but my assistant was supposed to check on hostile conditions, not me. It was that Peter WIIFM *(What's In It For Me)* rookie's fault, anyway—he left the bad trail in the first place. I knew he wasn't ready to scout yet—I heard it was his mother who pushed for his promotion and that weak HR manager who let him roll right over three other guys who had been waiting for that spot to open up for over a year. Oh—"

Both ants noticed Chris at the same time. Del Defoli-ant, the foraging manager, greeted him first, introducing Chris as that "weak" HR manager with a hint of a smile. Faultfinder hesitated, then mumbled, "Um, what I meant was . . . uh, well, it doesn't matter— at the end of the day, it's not my fault that others can't do their job right." He turned back toward Del. "And as for Peter WIIFM, somebody needs to give that Mama's boy some milk and cookies and send him home for a nap."

Chris greeted them, and then turned toward the complaining employee. "Why do you senior ants always refer to our younger generation as WIIFMs?"

Faultfinder responded, "It's because they all seem to have a WIIFM *(What's In It For Me?)* attitude." The grizzled looking ant had frown lines and furrows etched in his face from years of negative expressions.

Chris cleared his throat. "That's not just a characteristic of the younger generation. I know quite a few senior ants with the same attitude." He turned to Del. "Do you both have a few minutes?"

Faultfinder shrugged and nodded, following Del and Chris back toward the conference area. They entered a vacant room and sat down at one end of the long cherry table.

Chris sat down across from the wiry little ant and smiled sarcastically as he opened the folder, noting Connie's code name, *Aint to Blame.*

He looked up at Faultfinder, wondering why an ant, who had access to the very same benefits and advantages others enjoyed, would choose to ignore them and instead focus on everything negative. According to the surveys . . .

Faultfinder was making life miserable for everyone by criticizing others . . .

blaming teammates, over reacting, and picking apart every situation and project that he was involved in. No one wanted to work with him. He frustrated colleagues and supervisors alike with his habit of shooting down any plan proposed by others, and then failing to suggest a constructive alternative in its place.

After an initial discussion with Del and Faultfinder regarding the Employee Opinion Satisfaction Survey comments, Chris thought he would address some of the notes he had jotted down from Faultfinder's HR file that didn't seem to add up to his current standing.

"Hmmm . . . I see here that several years ago you were one of the most active squad leaders in your department. Your achievements in the Scent Trail Division are impressive, and many other departments have since adopted your advanced chemical communication protocols. I also see you came up for a promotion a while ago, but it was given to one of your teammates instead. Shortly after that, your reviews started going downhill fast. Would you like to tell me about that?"

The look on Faultfinder's face told Chris more than his words could, although Chris knew some of the facts already. There was anger and a clear sense of betrayal that he had worked so hard, yet did not win the prize he had made several attempts to win— a higher management position where he could spend more of his time on research rather than being out in the field. After a few moments, he responded with a snarl to Chris' question.

"I should have had that promotion, but instead they gave it to Slacker, who couldn't care less about improving communication during foraging expeditions. He just wanted to have one less boss and a better chance to blow off the few responsibilities he did have. Look at him now—he hasn't done anything since he's had that job, and his recruits don't even know what they're doing. His numbers are a mess. The food silos are at record low capacity, and the quality of the food they're bringing back is pretty pitiful, if you ask me."

Del interrupted him. "Faultfinder, have you ever considered that your lack of promotion may have something to do with the fact that your co-workers constantly avoid you so they can escape your criticism and non-stop complaining? Even if some of your observations about certain conditions or situations are valid, you might do better by trying to work toward seeing them improved—instead, your cup is always half empty and you make sure everyone knows it. Over the years, you've run off some of my best workers and you make the rest miserable along with you."

"And anyway, we're not here to talk about Slacker;

this is about you," Chris stated. "There's a real shake-up going on, and according to your co-workers, you are still a major part of the problem even though you have been approached about your attitude frequently in the past. Faultfinder, how do you see this? Can you tell me why so many employees are unwilling to work with you? And why you always blame everyone else and never take any *personal accountability?*"

"I don't know . . . I'm still taking teams out, but things are bad all over. We're not doing well since the leadership of our department hasn't given us any support or information on the best areas for foraging, and with more stunts like the one Peter WIIFM pulled, it'll just keep getting worse. If I was in charge, believe me, it would be a different story. But what can I do with the junk plans they're handing down to us? Hey, I figure it's my job to point out what's wrong since nobody else does. I'm just keeping them honest, right?"

"Well, Faultfinder, it's 'game over'—and nobody wins. You've blamed others long enough for your problems, but ultimately it's *you* who has to be accountable for what happens in your life.

"In the meantime, we must stop the infighting and negativity in this department. We've given you an opportunity to *take responsibility* for your actions, but you won't even accept liability for your involvement. So you leave us no choice but to remove the root cause of all the trouble. We have no choice but to let you go.

"Even after a lengthy process of feedback and solutions, prioritizing problematic areas, and agreeing on appropriate action plans to help you become more accountable, and coaching you on how to stop playing the blame game . . . we have all failed.

"Am I to understand you and your supervisor have already discussed this?" Chris solemnly asked.

They both nodded.

Chris turned to Faultfinder. "Hear me loud and clear, the GPS and Be-Attitude reads:

Accountability— Say NO to the Blame Game. Be accountable.

"Faultfinder, this is one guiding principle that will help you take charge of your life. It would help you tremendously if you accepted a few words of wisdom:

Let go of your past and start focusing on your future. You can't move forward in life always looking back into your rear-view mirror.

"One more thing: Your opportunity to be accountable starts right now."

Faultfinder stood up in frustration, "I have already put in my request to meet with upper management. If I'm going down, it won't be by myself. There are others to blame including Del . . . and you, too, Chris!"

Chris hadn't realized it was Faultfinder who had appealed to management, so he saw there was not much more he could do until he heard from them.

As Chris stood up, a strange sense of familiarity came over him, as if he had been part of this conversation before. "I understand that you will have your appeal, so we'll just wait and see how this all shakes out. Thank you both for your time today."

Chris hesitated for a moment, shook off the odd feeling, and headed toward the door.

How much time do you spend playing the blame game?

Are you a finger pointer?

Are you making life miserable for others by criticizing them?

10

Code Name: Change Resister
Aint Changing

Chris was thankful that he was almost finished with the day's mission. He had planned to talk with Change Resister last, a Big-Headed aint whose most recent contribution was creating a royal ruckus in the Military Department over the new manager Lieutenant Lena, who happened to be a little Carpenter Ant. The new leader came with impeccable credentials, was mentored by the former department head, and had been chosen after many rigorous interviews. But that didn't stop Change Resister and his buddies from trying to make life tough for her as she tried to implement new programs. Chris agreed again with Connie's observation that Change Resister should be called *"Aint Changing,"* as he recalled the aint's history of digging in his heels every time a new policy or procedure was implemented. Now, it seemed his influence over the other ants in the department was getting worse and creating constant turmoil. His influence was ruining otherwise good workers, and it had to be stopped.

Chris knocked on the manager's door, and she asked him to come in.

"Hi, Lena. Is Change Resister in?"

She shook her head. "I got your earlier message, but he hasn't returned from this morning's reconnaissance assignment. I do expect him back at any time for the meeting. Can I speak with you in the meantime?"

"Sure." He sat down and listened as she shared disappointing details about the recent battles taking place *inside* the Military Division.

"I just don't know why he is having such a problem working for me. I try my best to share my qualifications and background with all the ants and to let them know that I have worked my way up through the same school of hard knocks. Yet Change Resister and his gang of Big-Headed Ants seem to constantly fight against my directives. They are turning the whole Defense Department against me, and I've run out of ideas on how to handle the situation.

"They hate every new idea I try to share, and insist on using the same inefficient strategies for the military exercises. Because they're physically bigger, they think that they can bully everyone around here, including me."

Chris remembered some of the past complaints from Change Resister's co-workers and knew that this had been going on for quite a while, even before Lena had been installed as the new head of the department. Change Resister hated change. *Any* kind of change.

Just then, a commotion erupted outside her office, and they both knew Change Resister had returned.

Lena walked to the door and called him into the office, but he ignored her, continuing to joke with the other ants and acting as though he had not heard his name called.

Chris walked over to Change Resister to say hello.

"Yeah, hello," the aint said bluntly.

Chris asked him to join them in the department conference room.

Change Resister hesitated for a moment then followed Chris and Lena into the room.

They each took a seat at the long conference table,

staring at one another in awkward silence.

After initial small talk, and a couple of unsuccessful attempts to get Change Resister to openly share his thoughts, Chris leaned slightly forward and tried to reason with the huge ant.

"You know, I understand that change is hard. And I understand that it's easy to want to stay in a comfortable routine, one you know and perform well, but situations constantly change, whether we want them to or not.

Change is the one constant we can rely on.

"Sometimes, once we take that step into something new we come to discover that it is actually much easier than what we first believed. Each day, there is an opportunity to change a *turning point*—an event or incident that challenges you—into a *learning point* that can help you grow into a stronger, better ant."

Change Resister's large eyes narrowed as he folded his upper arms and sat farther back in his chair. "Hey,

what's this about? Is someone complaining about me?
Is this about her?"

He glared at Chris without looking over at Lena
and suddenly seemed especially defensive as he tried to
figure out why Chris was suddenly meddling in his
affairs.

"No, it's not about Lena. As you well know, she is
just the latest target in your personal war against
change.

"I'm here because you have been a constant and
serious stumbling block to progress for several departments and projects. For most of your tenure here,
Change Resister, you have built a reputation for drag-
ging your feet on every new procedure that we try to
put in place to make operations run more smoothly. It
seems like it doesn't even matter that we're trying to
help you. You reject ideas simply because they are not
the way you're used to doing things.

"Do you recall when we brought the efficiency
consult-ants in here last year?"

Change Resister rolled his eyes and smirked.
"Look, I didn't have time to walk them through everything that we do around here or go over equipment
operations . . ."

"That's right. You refused to work with them, which turned out to be a bad career move on your part. As a result, you don't know how to operate the new equipment we recently purchased to replace the outdated technology. Each decision you have made to resist the changes that are allowing our colony to progress has diminished your value to the team and put more of a burden on your teammates. Even if management and your co-workers had not identified you as a problem employee, you would eventually put the Military Department at risk due to your unwillingness to embrace change. *You* may have decided to stop learning and growing, but our competition never does.

"With budget cuts and fewer resources available everyone is being asked to step up and look within themselves at what changes they can personally make to help add more value to their team, their department, and to the organization. With you not being willing to embrace change, it's most likely you would create a dangerous or harmful situation at some point for the colony."

"Do you realize learning is a lifelong event?"

"Well, nothing has happened so far, and I don't know why we have to keep changing things anyway . . . if it ain't broke, why do we have to fix it? There's plenty to keep us busy without having to learn new things around here."

Chris scratched his head. "Your manager tells me she has tried everything to get you to see she's on your side, and that she wants to work with you—"

He finally just let it all out. "But she's a Carpenter Ant—everyone knows that their brains are smaller, and she just can't do the job as well as those of us who have larger brains. I don't care who trained her, or what great new ideas she's got. She hasn't proven anything to me or the guys, and we don't think she should be running this department," Change Resister sneered.

"Well," said Chris, "the truth finally comes out. Is

it really the size of her brain? I'm hoping that this is not about Lena being a Carpenter Ant or because this is the first time you've ever had to report directly to a female executive.

"This colony couldn't survive without its diversity. Isn't your best friend Hank, the guy in charge of the Scouting Team, a Red Ant? Is he less effective than Bob, who is a Brown Ant, because he's more detectable in the daylight? I don't think so. Isn't Annie, your wife, an Army Ant? Does she come to work looking for a battle or fight every day? I don't think so.

"I'm a Fire Ant. Does that fact automatically make me a bad candidate for HR director? Does that mean I'll come to work and bite my co-workers when I get upset? I don't think so, even though I can have a pretty painful bite.

"My goal has always been to help others to truly embody our GPS and embrace our Be-Attitudes. Change Resister, I think your problem may be fear, fear of the unknown. When people aren't willing to listen, learn, and change, they're not able to grow. They have a *hardening* of the heart that creates a *hardening* of the attitude. They become inflexible, just like you.

"You'd do well to remember that we are not born with an attitude of fear, but an attitude of power!"

Change Resister relaxed a bit in his chair and looked up at the ceiling while taking in and letting out a deep breath.

"I do know that I'm in violation of GPS 3—*refusing to embrace change and convert turning points to learning points.*" His voice softened, "My family and some of my co-workers have been telling me for a long time that I need to start embracing change. For me, it hasn't been fear of the unknown, but the fear of failure that has really paralyzed me—not knowing if I am going to be smart enough, or good enough to handle all of the new stuff that seems to be coming at me and my co-workers. It's just coming at us so fast," confessed Change Resister.

"I remember reading that *FEAR stands for False Evidence Appearing Real.* But every time fear shows up at my door, it sure appears real to me. But it's time, it's time right now. *I'm ready to walk by faith.* I'm ready to change right now—to embody the Be-Attitude of a Change Embracer. This is my new attitude, my new mindset. This is the new me, right now!

"I'm tired of disappointing those who depend on, and really care about me."

He turned to face Lena, "You work hard. We all know that. We also know you care about all of us and the welfare of the entire organization. I've just been too *fearful* and *selfish* to accept it. Is it too late to start over?"

Lena stood up and with a firm grip shook his hand. "Let's start over, right now!"

"From now on, call me Change Embracer."

Chris joined in for a group high-five.

"This worked out great! I really needed this! This is one report I'm looking forward to writing."

Chris snapped up his folder as he left the room, and walked back to his office thinking this day had been one of the longest in his career.

Still reeling from the day's events, especially the attitudes and disruptive antics of the unhappy aints, Chris knew he could not allow mental fatigue to overpower him. He still had to finish up the paperwork on the aints, and the senior management team was expecting a full written report on their desks first thing the following morning.

Chris sat at his desk rereading the surveys and files and going over his notes one last time. The situation was clear: The managers had repeatedly tried to get the aints to see their self-destructive behavior and dead-end ways, and in each case all but one *refused* to see the truth. The aints saw themselves as victims— unlucky, or unwilling, or even unable, to change.

Chris completed the necessary paperwork on each

of the employees, and rolled up his shirt sleeves to get down to the business of writing a comprehensive report about the lessons he'd learned during this long, challenging day.

He had plenty to report on, but he was still searching for the answer to The Chairman's question: *What is the difference between an ant and an aint?*

Are you a change resister?

Change is the power for growth.

In your life, what turning point have you converted to a learning point?

*Your attitude today determines
your success tomorrow.*

11
Wake-Up Call

The plane lurched sharply to the right as the pilot navigated through sudden turbulence. Chris' eyes flew open and his heart skipped a beat. *What the . . . ?* He grabbed the armrests. Jerked from his dream back into his shuddering aisle seat on Flight 1298, he was thankful that his seatbelt was still fastened.

He immediately looked down at his hands, which (to his great relief) were back to normal. He blinked and looked around slowly. Herman was buried in his newspaper. Chris sighed and leaned back as his breathing returned to normal, but his head was swimming with images and thoughts as he continued thinking about the reality he had just emerged from: ants, aints, bad attitudes, The Chairman, terminations, and reports. He tried to laugh at the craziness of it all, but somehow he couldn't shake it off. The dream was still larger than life in his mind. As the flight calmed down, he waited for the "fasten seatbelts" light to go back out, then he quietly slipped out of his seat and headed for the plane's restroom to freshen up.

Once inside, Chris stood before the miniature steel sink, looked at himself in the mirror, and froze.

Of course! Suddenly, he saw it, the significance of his dream.

Chris vividly recalled the details, especially the exchanges with each one of the aints.

Now I see them in a whole new light. It was easy for me to see how the aints were hurting others and limiting their own success with their attitudes, yet they couldn't see it themselves. Just like ME!

Every one of those aints represented one of MY bad attitudes, and how I refused to accept responsibility for my own lack of success.

I remember thinking if they could only see the damage their attitudes were causing them the way others did, they would change in a heartbeat. But they wouldn't.

Well, it may be too late for them, but it's not too late for me! I want another chance—I don't care what I walk into at headquarters. I am going to be accountable, speak the truth, and give my best. My team and company deserve better. My family deserves better, and so do I! I have a talented team, and yet I've brought out the worst in them.

I've kept them from succeeding because of my own *selfishness* and *bad attitude*. I've had the wrong mindset for a long time. My constant negative self-talk and self-criticism have led me to constantly criticize and put my team down. I clearly see how I've taken the fun out of the job, pushed them all away, and made things miserable around here.

What's been bugging me? . . . is ME!

But how did this happen to me? he wondered.

How did I allow *fear* and *selfishness* to overtake me? I know all this stuff. I read it years ago in Zig Ziglar's book *See You at the Top*. Zig rightly says, we all need a check up, from the neck up because we're all capable of having stinking thinking and getting hardening of the attitude. And, another book, *Attitude is Everything: 10 Life Changing Steps*, written by a guy whose name I wish I could remember, is based on a foundation of truth—*Guard* your ear gate by watching out for negative inputs; *monitor* your eye gate by renewing your mind; and *control* your mouth gate by remembering the tongue is the pen to your heart, knowing that the words you speak never die.

Both books had initially made a profound impact on Chris' attitude. He remembered that your *attitude* is the control center for your life, and your *heart* is the control center for your attitude.

Attitude and behavior are nothing but outward reflections of what is inside you.

All of Chris' problems had started to bug him because they were deeply rooted inside, which caused him to have a hardened *heart* and a hardened *attitude*. Over time, his unresolved issues had started to affect his behavior and performance.

"Excuse me, are you okay in there?" a concerned flight attendant asked through the locked door.

"Yes . . . yes, I'm fine," Chris replied, giving himself the once over in the mirror before opening the door.

Making his way past the waiting passengers, he bounded up the aisle eager to share his epiphany with Herman. Gone was his boredom and arrogance; along with his new tuned-up attitude, he had a newfound respect for his upbeat friend.

Chris sat down, took a sip of water, and launched into an animated description of his amazing dream. "But Herman, what was really weird about the dream was that none of the aints had regular names. They were all named after their bad behaviors: Free Agent—Aint on the Team, Faultfinder—Aint to Blame and Change Resister—Aint Changing, and everyone called them by their bad behavior names."

Herman scratched his head, paused, and said,

"Wow! This is powerful. The reason they were named after their behaviors is because when you name a behavior, it becomes real to you. And it's only then that you can start to change it."

Chris agreed and said, "It's time for me to take some personal accountability. My bad behaviors have been named, and starting right now my heart and attitude will be changed. I'm ready to turn my attitude . . . into action."

Their lively exchange lasted for the remainder of the flight to the delight of Chris' curious seatmate. The two men laughed and talked about their growing appreciation for the great wisdom of one of God's tiniest creatures.

We all need a check-up
from the neck up.

—Zig Ziglar

Do you need an attitude
tune-up?

Guard your heart,
it's the control center for
your attitude.

Our words set the course for our lives.

12
Meeting

"Hi Chris, I'm Jim. Can I get you some coffee or water?"

Chris politely thanked the vice president and sat down, settling in for the bumpy ride he was expecting. He told himself he just had to hold on, take his lumps, and convince Jim that he was not the same man who had been summoned to Dallas.

Jim was a bit tentative at first, trying to feel Chris out in hope of determining why his sales record had dropped so low, along with his reputation.

He went over each concern, yet Chris' responses were far different from anything Jim had been prepared for. Chris seemed to be filled with creative ideas and fresh new plans on how he was going to turn things around once he got back to the branch office.

The conversation confused Jim. He saw an excitement and positive approach that didn't line up with the negative feedback he had been getting about Chris over the past few years. Finally, when he couldn't stand the suspense any longer, Jim insisted on knowing why Chris seemed so dramatically different in person than on paper.

"Chris, I'm baffled. What happened to you to cause such a dramatic change in your attitude?"

Chris grinned and shook his head. "The story is too long to tell, but let's just say that I had a wake-up call very recently, where I learned how not to let the *aints* spoil life's picnic. I figured out what was bugging me—after years of grumbling and complaining about everything and everyone else.

"All my 'problems' had one common denominator—me."

"So I decided to *fire* my problems—each bad habit and attitude that worked against my success—and start letting my new habits and attitudes move me toward where I'd always wanted to go. The funny thing was, I never made the connection between my bad attitudes and resisting change, until I came face to face with them and finally saw the damage they were causing me. I realize that change is not change until *I* change.

"But believe me, everything's changed now. I can't wait to get back to the branch to get my new training ideas implemented and help get my team back on the right track.

"I finally see how I've led them down the same negative path that I was on. Regardless of how difficult it is right now, I'm going to encourage my team. We're going to work smart and I'm going to make sure that we have some fun! My focus will be not just to know our GPS and Be-Attitudes, but to start living them so they can help us navigate through and around our daily challenges, and help us reach our goals.

"It's not just what I'll say, but it will be the attitude behind my leadership that will make the greatest difference. It starts with *faith*, *confidence*, and *respect* for the individual. Respect for the individual starts with me respecting myself. I can do that daily by reminding myself that I have the ability to do great things.

Greatness starts with:

Teamwork: Living the Vision and having an attitude to Be Supportive; that leads to

Accountability: Saying NO to the Blame Game and always standing tall to Be Accountable; while understanding the importance of

Ethical Execution: Do What's Right Because It's Right, that gives us the power to Be Performance- and Integrity-Driven; and we should never forget—

We must always be willing to Embrace Change: While Converting Turning Points to Learning Points, by accepting our roles to Be Change Embracers.

We've got to Commit to Win: Do More Than is Expected, and always Be Coachable.

How important is Awareness: Notice What's Needed and Do What's Necessary? It reminds me every day to Be Responsible. And my personal favorite,

Attitude is Everything: If Something is Wrong Make It Right, never forgetting our job is to Be The Difference."

Jim got so pumped up, he started sharing some of his own thoughts about how the GPS and Be-Attitudes had played a key role in his personal and professional success. He encouraged Chris by offering to help him in any way he could to bolster his team's morale and to pull their sales figures up.

Chris smiled and thanked Jim for the meeting. He promised to call and follow up as soon as he got back home.

Walking away, Chris knew that strong teamwork, a positive attitude, and a *solid action plan* were going to be the foundation for his new leadership. But he didn't kid himself—he had a pretty big mountain to climb back home. He would have to take responsibility and undo a lot of damage he had done to the morale and expectations of his team. It probably wouldn't happen overnight. But somehow, he knew he could do it.

He realized as a leader, PRESSURE is a privilege.

He felt stronger and more confident than ever before.

Chris' plane ride back home was very different

from the trip out. No delays. No dreams. And no more anxiety.

He continued to reflect on the difference between *ants* and *aints*. He thought about Free Agent, Faultfinder, and Change Resister, and their selfless co-workers who understood the value of the colony's collective efforts. The life of the colony depended completely on the "higher nature" of the ants. Chris saw that each time aints chose to put themselves first, they brought the perfectly functioning team to a halt. They created disturbances and reactions that resulted in placing operations and, in extreme cases, even jobs and lives in jeopardy.

Chris turned the question over and over again in his mind. *What was the difference between the ants and the aints?*

Suddenly, he knew the answer.

Always lead with faith, confidence, and respect!

Fire your problems!

What creative ideas and fresh new plans will you take action on?

You help bring out the best in others
when you believe the best in them.

13
Speech—Part 2
"The A.N.T.S."

Chris took the large mahogany and silver plaque embossed with the names of each of his team members and held it up as a second roar went out from those listed on it. He thanked the emcee once more and cleared his throat.

"Thank you so much for this honor. This award represents far more than a year with good numbers. It represents a journey, and what people can do together when they choose to be part of something bigger than themselves. The real journey begins when you figure out *What's Bugging You*. If you would permit me, I'd like to take you briefly back to where it all started—in a world of ants—that inspired our division motto and the formula for our success: A.N.T.S.—which means **A**ttitudes **N**avigating **T**oward **S**uccess.

"There was a time I never dreamed that attitudes could really be so important in determining how high we could go in life. But then I did—*dream*, that is. And I haven't been the same since."

Chris proceeded to share his amazing dream with the audience, becoming more passionate in the telling as they responded with chuckles, grins, and nods of recognition as he colorfully described every scene in detail.

"When I returned to the branch office, I realized the role I had played in my staff being stuck in a deep rut. The dismal sales figures were the direct result of my own leadership—or lack of it. I knew if I could lead them *into* the rut, then I could lead them *out*. I knew it was going to be a challenge. I had to win their trust back, and they needed to know that I was sincere in my commitment, not only to them but to the entire organization. They had to work through some of their own stuff, just like I had to. Each one of us needed to make a few attitude adjustments to tear down old obstacles so we could begin to build something new together. It didn't happen overnight.

"The funny thing was that as we stayed focused on the task of building a strong team, the numbers somehow took care of themselves. I think we were all shocked when we learned that we had tripled our sales and landed in the top spot, when all we were hoping to do was to improve our internal communication and deepen our retail and dealer relationships.

"So what was the real secret to our division's success?

"I learned the answer from the ants and aints in that one life-changing dream. The only difference between an *ant* and an *aint* was one simple but powerful letter: the humble little *'I.'* I realized that the ants who were able to see that the choices *I* make, and the attitudes *I* choose to be lead by, determine the ultimate destination.

"The aints were unable to see it, which resulted in their getting in the way of their own success without ever realizing that *they were their greatest obstacle.*

"I saw how productive and fulfilled the others-centered workers were. They recognized that . . .

"being part of an achievement bigger than themselves gave their lives richness and meaning . . ."

that could not be found in the smaller world of those who were 'me' centered. It seemed so simple to an outside observer, yet sadly, it remained a mystery—no matter how many of us tried to point it out—to those who chose not to look beyond themselves for the answers.

"So how does that relate to my situation? I learned firsthand that anyone on any team or in any organization who ain't trying, ain't changing, ain't willing to do *that* job, ain't to blame, ain't ethical, ain't on the team, and ain't committed to win, is headed for failure. It's really that simple. What's more, I finally got it—that . . .

"I'm the one that makes the difference at the end of the day."

"It doesn't matter who else I think may be to blame, or in the way, or causing me to fall short of what I'm trying to do or who I'd like to be. I am the only one responsible for me, and the only one I can change. It's that simple. If anything else works for my good or helps me get where I am hoping to go, then it's a bonus and just one more reason to be encouraged and thankful with an *attitude of gratitude.*

"Above all else, guard your *heart* because it effects everything you do. Remember, you can't control what bugs you, but you can control how you respond to it. Once something is rooted in your *heart*, planted deep inside, it affects your attitude, behavior, and performance. It wasn't until I named the negative things that were affecting my heart—the aints—that they became real, and I was able to begin to change those things."

Chris was beaming as he shared each step of his past year's journey. He had each team member stand as he thanked them personally for their selfless efforts and renewed commitment. By the time he made his closing remarks, there was hardly a dry eye in the place. But Chris had one more surprise for the appreciative audience.

He introduced and thanked his special guest. Seated in the front row, Herman stood and saluted the crowd. Chris gave two thumbs up to his friend who had helped set him on a new course, and made sure that he would never, ever, look at ants the same way again.

"One last word before I go. We must live our GPS, letting them guide us and inspire us. We must model our Be-Attitudes. And then, we will always be like the ants—**A**ttitudes **N**avigating **T**oward **S**uccess!

"Have a *super-fantastic year!* Thank you very much!" Chris jumped off the stage and was instantly engulfed by a crowd of motivated colleagues and friends.

You are the only one responsible for yourself, and you are the only one you can change.

You can't control what bugs you, but you can control how you respond to it.

What's going to be your attitude adjustment?

You can't spell success without "U."

14
Closing

One of the most powerful words in the English language is attitude, because attitude—whether good or bad—is involved in everything you do, say, and believe. *Attitude is a choice*, and you are the only one who decides what kind of attitude you will wear on any given day.

So *What's Bugging You?* If you honestly ask yourself this question, how long would your list be? It seems as though something is always bugging people nowadays. Whether it's the economy, your marriage, your finances, your health, your job, a teammate, or even something as uncontrollable as the weather, the list of things that bug you can be endless.

However, when you allow something to bug you, you are choosing to put on the wrong attitude and this opens the door to becoming an *aint*. It's a matter of learning how to control the controllables. This begins

with a clear vision based on foundational principles
and Be-Attitudes that will guide you through the necessary steps of action needed to bring about results.

Guiding Principle Steps	Be-Attitudes:
Teamwork— Live the Vision	Be Supportive
Accountability— Say No to the Blame Game	Be Accountable
Ethical Execution— Do What's Right Because it's Right	Be Performance- and Integrity-Driven
Embrace Change— Convert Turning Points to Learning Points	Be a Change Embracer
Commit to Win— Do More Than is Expected	Be Coachable
Awareness — Notice What's Needed and Do What's Necessary	Be Responsible
Attitude is Everything— If Something is Wrong, Make it Right	Be the Difference

After spending several decades motivating others to maintain a super-fantastic attitude, I've noticed that it is far easier for people to recognize bad attitudes in others than it is to see those same attitudes in themselves. That's why I wrote *What's Bugging You?* as a parable. I'm sure you can name a Free Agent, Faultfinder, Change Resister, or another type of aint, where you work or live. However, if you are really honest with yourself, you might find that you have some of these same negative attitudes. I know I did.

I took some time to look back over my life and realized that when I allowed something—anything—to bug me to the point that it became rooted deep in my heart, I would soon develop a hardened *heart* and a hardened *attitude.*

Hardening of the heart affects a person's ability to *listen, learn, change,* and *grow,* and has a negative impact on your attitude, behavior, and performance. Sad to say, I know it did on mine. It wasn't until I recognized and named my bad behaviors—"the aints"—and worked toward removing the "I" that I was able to join the ranks of the A.N.T.S.—**A**ttitudes **N**avigating **T**oward **S**uccess. And now that you have read this book, I trust the same will happen for you.

I know that businesses, teams, and organizations today have procedures in place to appropriately manage poor performance. I started off this book by letting you know that it was written for your continuous improvement process to help you eliminate or better manage *What's Bugging You?* and to help you grow to an even higher level of success. My hope is that you are *now* well on your way!

Remember, your past may have impacted your present, but it does not dictate your future. You are predestined for greatness because *teamwork, change,* and a *winning attitude* . . . live within you!

"Take a lesson from the ants,
learn from their ways
and be wise."

—Proverbs 6:6

15
Aint Profiles

The stories you just read illustrate only three of the numerous aints we all encounter in our families, on our teams, and in the workplace. It would take several volumes to characterize all the types of aint behavior we deal with in our lives. But, you get the idea—for every aint there is a corresponding Guiding Principle Step (GPS) and Be-Attitude you can adopt to navigate through to success.

Code Name: Free Agent
Aint on the Team

The Aint Profile

General description:

Free Agents are people who do not choose to see the value of working with others. They often feel like they perform their jobs better than others on the team, which is why they feel compelled to question the qualifications and purpose of the team. They tend to make their own personal agenda the priority.

Free Agents often say:

- "You have to make your own way in the world and hope for the best. Who cares who gets hurt?"

- "I don't need anybody's help. I know what I'm doing."

- "I don't need the team. The team needs me."

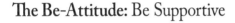

The Attitude Action

GPS (Guiding Principle Step) #1:
Teamwork—Live the Vision

The Be-Attitude: Be Supportive

The Attitude for Success:
The key to success for Free Agents is collaboration and getting everyone to see the importance of the roles they play. No one person is more valuable than the team. Free Agents may be very talented, but one of their top goals should be to make those around them better. When the team wins, everybody wins.

Code Name: Faultfinder
Aint to Blame

The Aint Profile

General description:

A Faultfinder is a person who criticizes and regularly finds reason to blame others and pick apart projects. They are finger-pointers, who tend to make life miserable for others. In the long run, Faultfinders tend to run people away.

Faultfinders often say:

- "I did my job. I blame this on my coaches, on management, and on the rest of the team."

- "I told you they didn't know what they were doing."

- "It ain't my fault. Someone else should take the blame."

The Attitude Action

GPS (Guiding Principle Step) #2:
Accountability—Say NO
to the Blame Game

The Be-Attitude: Be Accountable

The Attitude for Success:
The key to success for Faultfinders is accountability. Faultfinders should not concentrate on current or past problems, but focus on constructive solutions in order to make things better. They must also remember that when they point one finger at someone else, there will always be three fingers pointing back at them. So, three to one, Faultfinders will find the solution within themselves.

Code Name: Change Resister Aint Changing

The Aint Profile

General description:

Change Resisters regularly fight change. They are not comfortable with embracing new ideas. They drag their feet in adopting new procedures and reject concepts, processes, and technology that change the way they have to do things.

Change Resisters often say:

- "Why do we have to change it?"

- "If it's not broken, why don't we just leave it alone?"

- "Things are sure not like they used to be, none of these changes make any sense."

The Attitude Action

GPS (Guiding Principle Step) #3:
*Embrace Change—Convert
Turning Points to Learning Points*

The Be-Attitude: Be a Change Embracer

The Attitude for Success:
Fear of the unknown is the main reason why people don't embrace change. However, the Change Resister should recognize that change is the power for growth. The only difference between a rut and a grave is the dimensions. To encourage Change Resisters, always communicate the benefits of the transition to help them stay focused on the positive aspects of moving forward.

Acknowledgments

Thanks to Randy Melville, one of the best leaders I've ever worked with, and the entire Frito-Lay team, Winning Together . . . Everyday . . . I am also thankful to all the members of my A-Team (Attitude Team) and my airline companions for their help and support. I have an attitude of gratitude for all of you.

To my pastors, Dr. Creflo and Taffi Dollar, for making a positive mark on my life.

To the 1974 Garfield High School's Mens State Basketball Championship team, the undefeated Super Dogs, voted the Best Team in Washington state history. And to my greatest coaches, Fernando Amorteguy, Al Hairston, Ray Jones, and Lindsey Stuart.

To Les Brown, my first mentor and coach, thanks for teaching me "you're either on the way, or in the way."

To Garnett Campbell and Joann Canaday for your honest feedback, corporate HR experience, and all of your hard work.

To Arabella Grayson, excellent is an understatement for your work and dedication. No one knows me better and gets the most out of me. Sandy Bloomsfield, for your great insight, wisdom, and tremendous writing gift. To my sister, Toni Malliet, and others—I couldn't do it without Ramon Baez, Karen Beachy, a.k.a. MORE, Kacie Campbell, Jennifer Canzoneri, Paula Chance, Dianne Earley, Walt Floyd, Cheri Gillis, Jeffrey Gitomer, Cassie Glasgow, Yolanda Harris, Diana Harrison, Irie Jenkins, Clyde and Felecia Jones, Dawn Josephson, Sara Kahan, Meg La Borde, June Liggins, Cam Marston, Shannon Miser-Marven, Susan Oldham, Michele Rubino, Calvin Saunders, Fran Sims, Gayle Smart, Amie Smith, Janet Wagner, Desi Williamson, and Evangeline Ysmael.

Thanks to the number one management team, The SpeakersOffice. To Raytheon "Growth Through Innovation," keep up the super fantastic job. Finally, a special thanks to the whole team at Mid-America Apartment Communities for inspiring me with your guiding principles.

About the Author

Known across Corporate America for his energetic, innovative presentations, Keith Harrell is a dynamic motivational speaker who specializes in changing behaviors through a positive attitude. Keith shares his powerful messages, centered around attitude, change, teamwork, and leadership to audiences around the world.

The Wall Street Journal refers to him as a "Star With Attitude." The newspaper says, "What sets him apart from less successful speakers is driving ambition and an attitude that refuses to flag."

Keith earned his bachelor's degree in community service from Seattle University before embarking on a 14-year career with IBM, where he was recognized as one of the top sales and training instructors. Keith received the Certified Speaking Professional designation from the National Speakers Association and was inducted into the Speaker Hall of Fame, a lifetime award for speaking excellence and professionalism.

For your free attitude self-assessment, or to order your copy of the *What's Bugging You?* Workbook & Journal, go to www.superfantastic.com.

The Seven Guiding Principle Steps (GPS) and Be-Attitudes

Clip and save this reminder of the seven **Guiding Principle Steps (GPS)** and **Be-Attitudes** that will help you navigate through and around everyday challenges and to develop a *super-fantastic attitude.*

Accountability— Say No to the Blame Game	Be Accountable
Ethical Execution— Do What's Right Because it's Right	Be Performance- and Integrity-Driven
Embrace Change— Convert Turning Points to Learning Points	Be a Change Embracer
Commit to Win— Do More Than is Expected	Be Coachable
Awareness — Notice What's Needed and Do What's Necessary	Be Responsible
Attitude is Everything— If Something is Wrong, Make it Right	Be the Difference